Zach's Merry Xmas

Om KIDZ
An imprint of Om Books International

Om Kidz | Om Books International

Reprinted in 2023

Corporate & Editorial Office
A-12, Sector 64, Noida 201 301
Uttar Pradesh, India
Phone: +91 120 477 4100
Email: editorial@ombooks.com
Website: www.ombooksinternational.com

ISBN: 978-93-52760-37-4

Printed in India

10 9 8 7 6 5 4 3 2

Sales Office
107, Ansari Road, Darya Ganj
New Delhi 110 002, India
Phone: +91 11 4000 9000
Email: sales@ombooks.com
Website: www.ombooks.com

Zach's Merry Xmas

Paste your photograph here

My name is

Zach is very happy today. It is Xmas. He has been waiting for this day all **year.**

His Uncle **Zen** is coming over for **Xmas** dinner.

Zach has been **yelling Xmas** carols since **yesterday.**

The **Xmas** tree has been decorated. But the star is **yet** to be put on top.

Uncle **Zen** works in a **zoo**.
He feeds lions, tigers, leopards, **zebras** and all kinds of animals!

Zach is wearing his favourite **yellow** jacket. It has a **zipper** in the front.

He runs **zig-zag**

around the furniture.

Uncle **Zen** will be home soon. He will tell **Zach** a story about the **zoo.**

It is evening. **Zach** spends all day in the **yard** but Uncle **Zen** hasn't come **yet.**

Zach is bored waiting for Uncle **Zen.**

Zach's father says,
"Come with me **Zach.**"

"**Yes**," he says but his father knows that he is worried.

"Come, I will show **you** something," he tells **Zach.**

He takes **Zach** to the basement.

He pulls out an old box.

It has an old **xylophone** in it.
"This was my **Xmas** gift when I was a **young** boy like **you**," he says.

He spends all evening playing the **xylophone.** All of a sudden, someone sneaks from behind him and closes his eyes. **Zach** is amazed.

Zach turns around. It is Uncle **Zen.** What a surprise!

Uncle **Zen** has brought a toy **yacht** for him. This is going to be the best **Xmas** ever.

Know your words

Naming words

xylophone	yacht	zoo
Xmas	year	zebra
yard	zip	Zach

Describing words

yellow zig-zag

Doing words

yell

Sight words

yesterday	yes	young
you	yet	

Join the dots to show what Zach got for Xmas. Draw patterns on it and colour it.

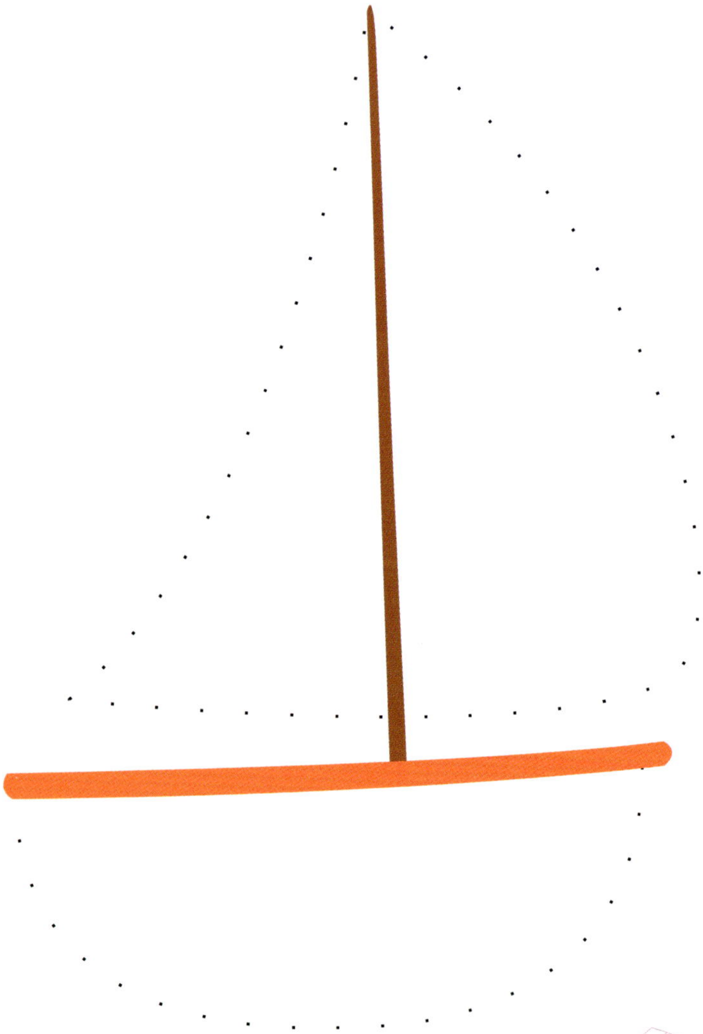

Find the below words in the word search.

W	A	O	U	R	K	Q	G
R	F	Z	Q	K	R	W	W
S	W	Y	E	K	M	J	Z
W	Q	A	A	B	X	J	O
X	M	A	S	C	R	S	O
B	N	G	V	S	H	A	T
Y	E	A	R	H	C	T	U
X	Y	R	O	C	F	K	N

XMAS

ZOO

YACHT

YEAR

ZEBRA

Colour the bubbles with words beginning with the letter 'z'.

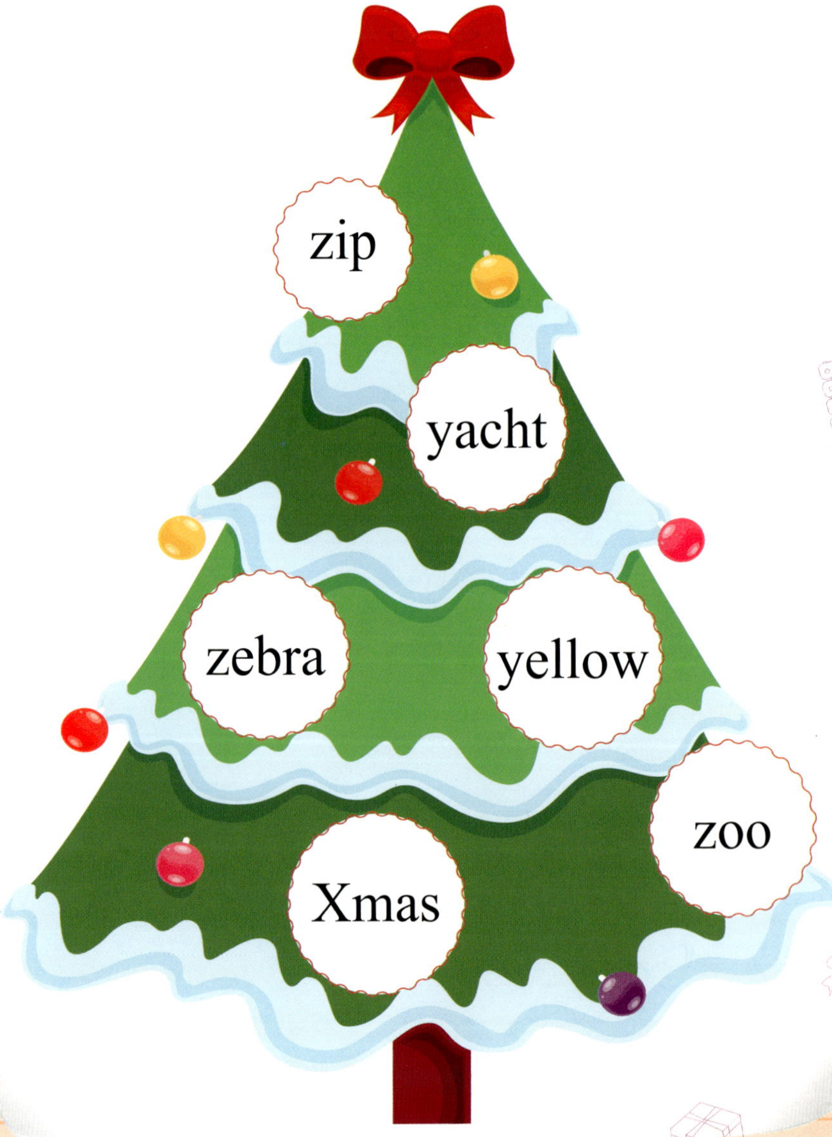